Sonja —

ICED

Winter, a hard
time to die. Enjoy!

JERRY PETERSON

DEDICATION

To Marge, my wife and first reader.

To the members of my writers group, *Tuesdays with Story*, sharp-eyed readers and writers who demand the very best of me in my storytelling and craft of writing.

To a friend and one-time colleague who prefers to remain unnamed.

ACKNOWLEDGMENTS

This is the sixth book I've published as indie author, the fourth under my Grand Medallion Books imprint.

We indie authors depend on a lot of people to make our stories and books the best that they can be. Dawn Charles of Book Graphics, a superb cover designer, worked with me on this volume.

A knock-out cover is vital to grabbing potential readers and so are the words on the back cover that say this book is one you really ought to buy. For those words, I turned to Chicago crime writer Michael Black. Mike has written a much taller stack of mysteries and private eye novels than I have. He even wrote two with now retired Law & Order: SVU star Richard Belzer.

I always close with a note of appreciation to all librarians around the country. They, like you and your fellow readers who have enjoyed my James Early mysteries, my AJ Garrison crime novels, and my short story collections have been real boosters. Without them and you, there would be no reason to write.

A NOTE FROM THE AUTHOR

Iced came into the world as a thumb novel. Remember those?

Thumb novels were the rage a decade or so ago. Not here, but in Japan.

Japanese teens were tapping out novels on their cell phones, using their thumbs on the keypad. Thus thumb novels. Tens of thousands of novels a year.

The hallmarks are short paragraphs and short chapters because your reader is going to read your novel as a serial, perhaps a chapter a day, on his or her cell phone's screen.

The idea intrigued me. So, for a challenge, I decided to see whether I could write a thumb novel. I hedged and wrote on my computer–a bigger keyboard–but stuck to the dictum of short paragraphs, short chapters, short book.

When I took my chapters to my writers group for critiquing, one of my colleagues read them on her cell phone's screen and reported to our group that, yes, it can be done.

I had long wanted to write a thriller, and the thumb novel was my opportunity.

I set my story in Wisconsin in the winter. In this way, the weather would be one of the hazards with which both the hero and the villain would have to contend.

Short Death was the working title. I didn't like it, so Millie Mader, one of my writers group colleagues, said I should call the novel *Iced.* Perfect, I said, because one of the chase scenes takes place on a frozen lake, on the ice.

No, said Millie, your killer murdered two people. He 'iced' them.

So Millie's title is fitting for two reasons.

I published *Iced* online four years ago, on Textnovel.com.

What you are about to read is updated version of that story. Gone are several references that were right for 2009, replaced with references that are right for today. One example, in the 2009 version, Wads sees a McCain/Palin bumper sticker. In this version, it's a Romney/Ryan bumper sticker.

ALSO BY JERRY PETERSON

Early's Fall, a James Early Mystery, book 1. . . . "If James Early were on the screen instead of in a book, no one would leave the room."
– Robert W. Walker, author of *Children of Salem*

Early's Winter, a James Early Mystery, book 2 . . . "Jerry Peterson's *Early's Winter* is a fine tale for any season. A little bit Western, a little bit mystery, all add up to a fast-paced, well-written novel that has as much heart as it does darkness. Peterson is a first-rate storyteller. Give *Early's Winter* a try, and I promise you, you'll be begging for the next James Early novel. Spring can't come too soon."
– Larry D. Sweazy, Spur-award winning author of *The Badger's Revenge*

The Watch, an AJ Garrison Crime Novel, book 1 . . . "Jerry Peterson has written a terrific mystery, rich in atmosphere of place and time. New lawyer A.J. Garrison is a smart, gutsy heroine."
– James Mitchell, author of *Our Lady of the North*

Rage, an AJ Garrison Crime Novel, book 2 . . .
"Terrifying. Just–terrifying. Timely and profound and even heartbreaking. Peterson's taut spare style and truly original voice create a high-tension page turner. I really loved this book."

– Hank Phillippi Ryan, Agatha, Anthony and Macavity winning author

A James Early Christmas and *The Santa Train*, Christmas short story collections . . . "These stories are charming, heart-warming, and well-written. It's rare today to see stories that unabashedly champion simple generosity and good will, but Jerry Peterson does both successfully, all the while keeping you entertained with his gentle humor. This should definitely go under your tree this season."

– Libby Hellmann, author of *Nice Girl Does Noir*, a collection of short stories

ICED

A JOHN WADS CRIME NOVELLA
BOOK 1

CHAPTER 1

JOHN WADKOWSKI sat at The Library's bar, his favorite watering place in downtown Jamestown, noodling with his Samsung Galaxy. On the screen the word *magistricide*, meaning the killing of a teacher or master. He clicked "adopt," committing himself to saving the word from the scrap heap of vocabulary neglect. Wadkowski swivelled the phone's screen around to the bartender, Barb Larson, a redhead in a black mini-skirt and the tightest of rust sweaters.

She read it as she continued polishing a pilsner glass. "So where you gonna use that word?"

"Dunno. Just find it interesting."

The phone jumped with the University of Wisconsin fight song. Wadkowski clicked off the Save The Words website and the ring tone, glanced at the caller ID, and put the phone to his ear.

"Wads," came the voice of Howard Zigman, a friend with the Wappello County Sheriff's Department, "I hate to be the bearer of bad news."

"I'm sitting down, so go for it."

"Your Iraqi buddy, Raheem Naseri?"

"What about him?"

"He's dead."

"My God, no."

"Looks like suicide."

"Where?"

"You're not going to believe this. Back in the woods on your old farm....Wads?"

"I'll come out."

Wads slipped the phone in his pocket as he pushed off his stool. He wagged a finger at the bottle he had been nursing. "Am I good for that?"

"Two bucks seventy, I guess. I don't know why you drink that stuff. Nobody else does."

"Muscle Milk. It's the old dairyman in me, and, hey, bodybuilders love it."

He shagged on outside where the cold of February slapped him, the afternoon shadows already stretched long. At the curb, with still a half-hour on the parking meter, stood the one thing he had come away from his farm sale with free and clear, his Chevy Silverado dually with the biggest diesel engine in it the company made. He'd bought the truck when milk hit twenty dollars a hundredweight. It had tumbled to half that when the economy went to hell. And his debt, his advisor at the Farm Credit agency said sell out and go do something else.

He did and took an efficiency in town, but there was nothing else to do. The city police, the sheriff's department, the state police all had hiring freezes, and he had, as a former military police investigator, the credentials for anything they might have. All he could get was assistant manager/night shift at the Main and Bypass Kwik Trip.

Wads fired the engine. He drove out of town, west toward the farm and fields of bad memories. He brought out his cell, pressed "contacts," and scrolled down to Raheem Naseri–his home phone number. Wads tapped on the number. Shatha should be there, but no answer.

He scrolled to the nursery school where she worked and again tapped on the number. On the third ring: "Cradles to Crayons. Debbie here."

"Debbie, this is Wads. Shatha there?"

"She didn't come in today."

CHAPTER 2

HE SAW THEM from the top of the rise on the county road, the pulsing emergency lights of a flock of patrol cars and one lone ambulance.

Wads drove on. As he got closer, he decided the best place to leave his truck was the ditch, so he pulled off and parked behind a state police cruiser. He rescued his parka from behind the passenger seat and walked into a patch of shagbark hickories. A deputy, with the collar of his winter jacket up around his ears and dragging on a cigarette, stopped him.

"Let him on," a man further into the woods called out.

Wads stuffed his hands in his pockets and rambled on. "A few more uniforms and you could hold a convention," he said when he came up beside a plainclothesman hunched against the cold—Howard Zigman, a sheriff's detective.

"We do turn 'em out for shootings." Zigman thumbed at the trooper standing nearby. "Know this man?"

Wadkowski stuck out his hand. "John Wadkowski. Most people call me Wads."

The trooper, a tall man, spade black, neck thickly muscled, clapped onto Wads's hand and gave it a smart shake. "Sam Dixon. Just transferred to this district."

"You'll do well here. So who found him?"

Zigman stamped his feet, to pound some warmth into them. "Marty Walton, your old neighbor. He was driving by and saw the car in the woods. He knew it wasn't right, so he walked in, saw the mess, and called Nine-One-One. Naseri's on the other side of the car."

The car–an old Kia, small and cheap. Wads's church bought it after Wads told them the new family needed help, a family he had sponsored. He had known Naseri in Iraq. The man had been an interpreter for Wads's unit, and when he finally got visas for himself, his wife, and their little girl...

Zigman and Dixon led the way around to where a technician in sheriff's department coveralls and plastic gloves was swabbing for something–the tech, a woman Wads didn't know.

Naseri, on the ground, laid back against the driver's door, his head to the side, a small hole apparent in the right temple but little blood, a pistol to the side of the body.

Zigman motioned at the gun. "Your classic Saturday night special. Know he had it?"

"Yeah. I couldn't talk him out of it. He said people hassled him when they found out he was a Muslim. I told him if he'd just go by Ray–Ray Naseri, not insist on Raheem–nobody'd be the wiser."

"There's no understanding prejudice. Didn't he attend your church?"

"For me, yes, but his spiritual home is–I'm sorry, was–the As-Sunnah mosque in Madison. Any chance this could be murder?"

"Wads, I don't see it. Sam and I've walked the area. No signs that there's been anyone else here. But with the ground dry and frozen–"

The technician, kneeling beside the body, held up a pad to Zigman. "I've got gunshot residue on his right hand."

Zigman turned to Wads. "I'd say that cinches it, wouldn't you?"

Wads grimaced.

Zigman stared at him. "Okay, give, what's the problem."

"Raheem was left-handed."

"Left-handed? You're sure of that?"

Wads rubbed at the back of his scalp. "We were joined at the hip for a year."

"Damn, this changes things. You're an old Army investigator, who'd you look at?"

Wads peered through the window of the Kia. "Anything in there?"

"Nothing of interest. I'll give you an inventory after we're finished."

"Sure." He stepped over to a tree stump. There, before he sat down, he brushed away hickory shells squirrels had shucked. "We've got a few knotheads who hang out at that bar on the far side of the lake. I see 'em when they gas up at the Kwik Trip. Foul-mouthed. To hear them talk, they'd castrate anybody who's not like them."

Trooper Dixon pitched up an eyebrow. "How's that?"

"White guys. A suggestion, if you ever go in that bar, don't go in alone. And carry a baseball bat."

Zigman scribbled something in his notepad. "A single shot and clean, this doesn't look like a hate killing to me."

"Still I'd check it out."

"So who else?"

"Howard, I don't know."

"Work maybe?"

"I got Raheem a job in the auditing department at the Fifth Street Bank. Who's going to get mad at a man who pushes numbers from nine to five?"

"Somebody at his mosque?"

"You're thinking they're running a school for terrorists up there, that they've got a Jehadi who hates Ray because he worked for us?"

"We shouldn't pursue it?"

Wads massaged his face. He'd gotten up too early. "I guess, but, jees, Howard, be careful."

"Hey, I was in the Guard over in the sandbox. I know the sensitivities, but I also know the hatreds among the sects and the clans. If you don't like that one, let me try this out on you, could it be that someone wants his wife?"

To Wads, that didn't calculate either.

Zigman flipped back a couple pages in his notepad. "First things first then. I've got a Bratsburgh address for the family—husband, wife, and daughter—

daughter age six. We better go see the wife and break the news."

"I called on the way out. No answer."

"Maybe she and the girl are home by now." The detective pulled a portable radio from his coat pocket. He pressed the transmit button. "Connie, Zigman here."

"Go ahead."

"I'm going to Bratsburgh, to the home of the deceased. The death notification."

"Bratsburgh? What's the address?"

"H Street, Two-Fifteen."

"Howard, Nine-One-One's just dispatched fire trucks there. They say the house is burning like the devil's furnace."

CHAPTER 3

ZIGMAN AND WADS strode from their vehicles past a television newswoman videotaping the inferno, the stench of the fire drifting their way. They went on to a Bratsburgh VFD fire engine pumping a jet of water up onto the roof, to the fire chief gesticulating at her second-in-command. That man ran off toward another fire crew.

Zigman crowded into the chief, Char Kranz, a stout woman in full bunker gear, her glasses streaked by ash. Wads hung off to the side, the three of them shielding themselves from the heat of the blaze by staying on the near side of the truck.

Zigman stabbed a finger at Kranz's cigar. "Smoking on the job, chief?"

She puffed away. "Keeps me calm."

"But there's a fire here."

"So, you gonna have my boys douse me?"

He shook his head.

Kranz waved Wads over. "I can see why Ziggy's here, but how about you?"

"I know the family."

"The Naseris? Damn shame, isn't it?"

"Anyone inside?"

"If there is, they're done crispy by now. We won't know 'til we get the fire out an' get in there."

Zigman jerked his head toward the blaze. "Cause?"

"Jesus, you ask the impossible."

"How about a guess then?"

"Could be a grease fire in the kitchen. Electrical maybe. But more likely they couldn't afford the winter gas bills. Went out an' got themselves a kerosene heater at the Home Depot, you know, figuring to save a little money, trying to get by 'til spring. Those damn things are house fires waiting to happen. I got me a call into the state fire marshal."

Wads peered around the end of the truck. "Roof's about to fall in."

Kranz, her cigar jammed in the corner of her mouth, waddled around for a look. "Basement in that house, do you remember?"

"Yeah."

"Then the floor's gonna go, too. We'll have us one big water-soaked ash pit. It's gonna be a helluva mess to prod through."

The front wall buckled. With its movement came the squall of nails pulling away, and the roof caved. Ash and sparks billowed out. Wads brought his sleeve up over his mouth and nose, to keep the smoke out.

The floor gave way, and in the wink of a cat's eye the burning house dropped from sight.

Kranz turned away from the fire, to Wads. She studied the burn on the end of her cigar. "That's all she wrote."

A blast threw Kranz to her knees and Wads onto his side, a blast that sent floor joists and timbers high and debris wide. A shower of burning shingles rained down.

Kranz scrambled through the jumble of smoldering trash and grabbed hold of Wads. She beat at his burning hair, he doing his best to fight her off.

"Stop that, Wads! You're on fire."

He heard the fire chief, but only barely, as if her voice were dribbling out the end of a garden hose. The blast had been deafening. When what she said registered, he whipped his hands back over his scalp—flailing, rubbing. He smelled it, the singed hair.

Kranz got a good grip on Wads's ears, made a quick visual of his head. "Man, your barber's gonna have one helluva time shapin' you up. You're just damn lucky your brain didn't cook."

"What?"

"I said—oh never mind."

"You see my cap?"

Kranz turned him and pointed toward a muddy puddle on which floated a baseball cap.

Zigman rescued it, the cap emblazoned with a Jamestown Ice Hogs logo. He wrung out the dirty water while he strolled back. Zigman handed the cap over, and Wads reshaped it before he slapped it on his head.

"Wet like that, you're gonna freeze yer dome," Kranz said.

"Huh?"

"I said you're gonna freeze yer dome!"

"Oh. I'll risk it."

"Don't say I didn't warn you."

Zigman stared at Kranz. "The explosion, didn't you cut off the gas line?"

She parked her knuckles on her ample hips and gave the detective a smoldering look that said what do you think I am, some dumb yahoo?

"First thing we do when we roll up," she said through gritted teeth, "is cut the damn gas valve at the curb. And if the electric company's breaker doesn't cut the juice to the house, we haul down the powerline."

"Did you do it?"

"'Course, we did."

"Then what caused the explosion?"

"That's for the fire marshal to figure out, wouldn't you say? I gotta go check on my guys."

Kranz tramped off, leaving Zigman and Wads in the shelter of the pumper. Zigman leaned in. "You all right?"

Wads massaged an ear. "Other than I can't hear too well."

"Remember that television reporter when we came up?"

"Videotaping the fire, sure."

"I'm thinking the fire marshal's going to want her tape—I sure would—to see what happened as it happened."

"We'd better find her, huh?"

Zigman motioned for Wads to follow him.

They picked their way through the debris, moving back the way they had come, Wads the first to see her. He broke into a run. He leaped across a burning timber and went down on his knees, next to the woman in a parka, twisted, lying on her side, a jagged piece of two-by-four protruding from her chest.

Wads pressed his fingers on the artery in the woman's neck. His shoulders slumped. "This one's for the coroner, not the EMTs."

Zigman whipped out his radio and squeezed the transmit button. "Connie?"

"Go ahead."

"Call Ben out at the woods. Tell him we need him at the house fire."

"What happened?"

"The whole damn thing went up in the biggest explosion. Killed a TV reporter."

"Oh Lord, do you know who?"

"Just a minute." Zigman hunkered down next to Wads. "Is that an ID there?" He nodded at a card on a lanyard by the deceased's shoulder.

Wads turned the card over. "Issued by the station. Tamara Donaldson, WISN."

Zigman brought his radio back up. "A Tamara Donaldson. Must be new. I've not seen her before. Madison Channel Three. Call them for me and suggest they send somebody down."

"Consider it done."

Zigman slipped his radio back into his coat pocket. "It was such a fine day this morning."

"Tomorrow's gotta be better." Wads pointed away. "Camera's over there. It's the new type—all digital. What you want is the memory card."

"How do you know so much?"

"Eddie Thoms gave me a lesson at The Library. He worked Three's Jimmytown bureau until he took a job in Iowa last week."

"So you don't know this one?"

"No. Probably just out of college. Hire them cheap at Three they do." Wads peeled back the cuff on the sleeve of his parka. He peered at his watch. "Kwik Trip calleth. I've gotta get to work."

"You're going to leave me with this mess?"

"Howard, get me hired and I'll be glad to stay, but until then, selling gasoline and Mars bars pays the rent for me."

Zigman made a turnaround. He took in the full scene as if for the first time. "So what have I got here? A murder at your farm that may or may not be connected to this house fire, a fire caused by nobody knows what, and the death of a young woman that shouldn't have happened."

Wads tapped his ear. "Add this to your list, a guy who can't hear too good."

He walked off toward his truck. Wads stopped at a scorched coaster wagon on the way. Were Shatha Naseri and her daughter in the fire? Wads picked up the wagon. He ran a gloved hand over the damage. Maybe they'll want this if they weren't. Wouldn't take much to clean it up.

He spotted a doll that had been flung wide and picked that up, too.

At his truck, Wads lifted the cover on the box and laid the wagon and the doll inside. Could that be one of those Bratzillaz dolls? Whatever happened to Barbie? He secured the cover and went around to the driver's door, the door bashed in and the window shattered. A blackened toilet laid on the ground.

Now how'm I gonna explain this to my insurance man?

CHAPTER 4

WADS, FLASHLIGHT IN HAND, read the gallonage off pump eight and wrote the numbers on his inventory sheet. A Cadillac stationwagon thumped in over the cracks in the concrete driveway as he turned the beam on the numbers on pump nine.

"Get a little service here?" came a husky voice from the wagon.

Wads continued his inventory. "It's you-pump at this place."

"Aw, come on. Have pity on an old lady, wouldjah, honey?"

Wads stepped around the pump. He leaned his elbow through the driver's window and hunkered down, to get a look at this helpless soul. Surprise lit his face. "Kranz?"

"Understand your truck got damaged out at the fire."

"Yeah, the door got pretty well bashed in."

"Well, I'm here to help you."

"How's that?"

The Bratsburgh fire chief brushed Wads back as she opened the door and stepped out of her car. She wore a purple fedora at a rakish angle, a storm coat, slacks with a crisp crease showing below the coat's hem, and low heels.

Wads admired the woman. "You clean up pretty good."

"Blow the smoke off me and I'm not half bad." Kranz reached back in her car and brought out a leather portfolio. "Tonight I'm your friendly neighborhood insurance adjuster."

"I knew you messed with insurance, but I never guessed this."

"Yup, work for myself. LaPrairie Mutual called me, so here I am. Where's the truck?"

He motioned toward the side of the building.

"Let's take a look, shall we?" she said and led the way. "So what hit it?"

Wads pulled out his cellphone. He tapped a photo up on the screen and held it over for Kranz to see.

"A toilet? Well, flung out by the blast, that'll sure do it." She bent a bit at the waist, the better to study the door panel, caved-in. "See you duct-taped some plastic for a new window."

"Darn cold driving into town without any glass, I'll tell you."

"Can you open it?"

"What?"

"The door."

"No, it's jammed. I have to get in and out the passenger door."

Kranz straightened up. She wriggled her fingers for the flashlight, and Wads gave it to her. She played the beam up one side, over, and down the other side of the door's edge. "Frame's not damaged, so you're in luck on that part. New door and glass, door painted to match your truck, we're looking at thirteen, fourteen hundred dollars, and you've got a thousand bucks deductible."

"At least the insurance will pay the rest."

"I wouldn't turn in a claim if I were you."

"Why not?"

"LaPrairie will pay, but they'll dingly-damn sure come back on you and up your premium, stiff you three ways from Sunday."

Wads gazed at the bashed door on his pickup. "So I gotta eat the expense?"

Kranz got a good fire going on a fresh cigar. She blew a ring of smoke to the side. "I'd do it. Look, every farmer I know is a mechanic. Get yerself a door at the junkyard, put it on, and make a deal with Herb over at the Dedenter shop to use his place and paint it yourself. You can get by with maybe two hundred bucks outta your pocket."

"Two hundred I don't have versus a thousand I don't have, some choice."

"Wads, you can drive your truck as it is. Your passenger door works, so you're all right."

"But my driver's door, it's a shameful mess."

"Uh-huh, like my partner's truck. She never fixes anything, which is good for me because she leaves my Caddy alone."

WADS SLASHED HIS BOX CUTTER along the top of a carton of Huggies, then busied himself stocking a shelf with packages.

"Boss," called out the high school teen at the cash register.

"Yeah, Cindy."

"You should come see this."

He glanced over at the six-foot-four brunette in a Kwik Trip smock waving to him. Wads liked her, hired her because he knew no one would try to buffalo a woman of her altitude. Shoplifting had dropped to zero on her shift. He tucked the last of the Huggies onto the shelf and trotted up the aisle. "Whatcha got?"

She aimed a long finger at the front window. "Eight bikers at the pumps. Look, they're all filling at the same time."

"They swipe their cards?"

"Tapped the 'pay inside' buttons."

Pump one clicked off on the light board next to the cashier, then three, five, seven, and the rest. The motorcyclists twisted the gas caps down on their tanks and, on a signal from a guy in a spiked German helmet at the farthest pump, all threw a leg across their saddles and roared away.

Wads grinned. "Cute. Gas theft. I love it. Did you get any license plates?"

"No, and the video system's down."

"Okay, hon, here's what you do. You call Nine-One-One and tell 'em what happened. They'll have four police cars out here before you hang up."

"That's it?"

"Nope." Wads dashed back to his office. He came out, pulling on his parka. "I know who those guys are and where they're going."

He slapped a business card on the counter as he backed his way toward the front door. "Three minutes, call that number. It's a sheriff's detective. You tell Howard to get a couple deputies out to the Owls' Club, and they can have themselves a party arresting the gas thieves."

CHAPTER 5

WADS SAT IN HIS TRUCK at the top of a hill, the
engine idling. He peered through night-vision
binoculars he'd liberated from Uncle Sam at the end
of his hitch in Iraq.

"Jake, Jake, Jake," he murmured, "you shouldn't
make it so easy."

In the glasses, a dozen motorcycles parked in
front of the Owls' Club, a tavern on the backside of
Kandiyah Lake, eight of the bikes clustered together,
all leaning away from him.

Wads rummaged his Army nine-mil from the
glove box. He shoved the gun in his waistband, then
eased the truck down the hill and onto the flat of the
county road, the chunky cinder-block building
growing in his windshield, the neon sign beckoning
thirsty souls inside for a Miller's or a Rolling Rock.
He cut his headlights short of the club's gravelled lot
and rolled in, the air tainted by engine exhaust and
beer. Wads punched the number of the tavern into
his cell.

On the third ring, a rumbly voice answered.

"Is Jake Karns there?" Wads asked.

He heard the voice on the other end shout, "Karns! Call for you." In the background, Nine Inch Nails' Trent Reznor screeched away on "Survivalism."

Some moments went by before a new voice came on, asking, "Yeah?"

"Jakey boy. This is Wads. You where you can see out the front window?"

"So?"

"Watch the show." He clicked off and, with a ballet of movements, pulled on the headlights, slipped the transmission into first, and drove forward. He banged and bounced over one motorcycle after another until eight laid in ruins. Wads then floored the accelerator. The dual rear wheels sprayed gravel as the truck rocketed sideways and slid to a stop beyond the tavern's front door.

Wads bailed out. Gun in hand, he plastered himself against the wall as the door whammed open and a squat, bald man in leathers ran out, others behind him.

Wads grabbed the lead man's collar. He yanked him back, jammed his pistol in the man's ear, and bellowed at the others, "Kiss the dirt or old Jake gets a killer of an ear ache!"

Karns sneered. "You don't have the balls."

Wads flicked his gun away and whipped it back hard, the blow snapping Karns's head to the side. The yell said pain.

Wads again jammed the barrel in Karns's ear. "Boys, are those sirens I hear?"

Several of the bikers twisted in the gloom of the parking lot. They stared over their shoulders at distant lights and sound coming their way.

"That's sheriff's deputies, boys. They're coming to take your butts to jail or your buddy's body to the morgue, your choice. Down on your knees. Now."

Two of the larger men, built like Green Bay Packer linemen, stepped forward. As they did, they brought out pistols of their own.

Wads gave them the cold eye. "Bad choice."

Karns raised a fist. "Kill the bastard, and shoot me if you have to to do it."

Wads racked back the hammer on his gun.

CHAPTER 6

TREMBLING, Wads leaned against the shower wall in his apartment, the water roiling down, flushing away the soap but not the harrowing moment at the Owls' Club.

Too close.

Too damn close.

He shook his head to rid his memory and swiped soppy hair up out of his eyes.

Enough of this.

He turned the hot water off. Wads stood for a bit–dripping, the bathroom infused with the scent of Irish Spring–before he reached out through the curtain for a towel. A hand put one in his hand. He felt fingers touch his, and Wads jerked his head out through the curtain. A woman, barefoot and in his Packer Backer bathrobe, stood before him.

"Where the heck—"

"Your spare key." Barb Larson gave him a radiant smile. She held the key out, and she also held out a glass. "Rum and Coke?"

"Don't like rum. Don't even have any."

"That's why I brought my own." She savored the drink in a way that said something better, far more warming, was in the offing. "Hon, you were so miserable at last call, I figured you could use a little company."

He pulled the towel inside and rubbed down. "I came within a calf's eyelash of blowing a man's head off tonight."

"You didn't say anything earlier."

"Didn't wanna talk about it."

"But you didn't do it, right?"

"Huh-uh." Wads wrapped the towel around his waist. He felt a draft. Before he could turn, hands slid down under his towel to his groin—fingers, soft and warm. They encircled his penis as Larson leaned into him.

"I'd say you're ready, big fella."

"Barb."

She, now naked, turned him to herself and guided his penis in, between her legs.

He flushed, his breath quickening.

"Come on, cowboy, you can do it."

A rapping came at the apartment door.

"Ignore it."

"But—"

The rapping continued, more insistent.

"Somebody—"

She wrenched the shower faucet on, but the sound from the door cut through the spray.

Wads twisted himself free. He stumbled out of the shower and grabbed up a fresh towel and the robe Larson had dropped, the rapping demanding that someone come. Wads stepped into his slippers. He went to the door, pulling on his robe as he hustled along. When he got there, he squinted through the peephole. "Shatha?"

"Mister Wadkowski, I have to see you."

Wads opened the door.

Shatha Naseri stood before him, a petite, olive-skinned woman, lost in a full-length quilted coat and keffiyah. She glanced at his feet. "Why are you wearing bunny slippers?"

"A niece, she gave them to me. But you didn't come here for that."

"My Raheem, he's dead, isn't he," she said, her eyes red and filled with sorrow.

Wads took hold of the woman's elbow. He drew her inside and closed the door. "Where in God's creation have you been?"

The confusion in her eyes suggested the woman was grasping at loose ends and not doing well. "Madison," she whispered. "Raheem said little Afraima and I had to leave. He was afraid."

"When?"

"This morning–yesterday morning."

"Afraid of what?"

"He would not tell me. I borrowed our neighbor's car, took Afraima to the mosque. When we came back, our house was burning. I knew then, so I took Afraima to friends, and I have been driving around since. Raheem said I should see you."

"Of course. How about I make you some tea?"

Shatha Naseri studied her hands. "How many times have we had tea together, you, my Raheem, and I?"

Wads scuffed away to the kitchen. He turned the burner on under a saucepan of water and rifled through a cabinet until he found a box of tea. "All I've got is Red Zinger."

"You Americans, you can never have just black tea."

"Right, we've got to juice it up."

Barb Larson came out of the bathroom dressed in a tight sweater and short skirt, her bartender's outfit.

Wads, when he saw her, dropped the box. "Shatha," he gabbled, "this is Barb Larson, a friend. Barb, Shatha Naseri."

"I know. I heard." Larson went to Naseri and took her hands. "I am so sorry for what happened."

"You knew my Raheem?"

"No, but Wads has always said nice things about him, and you, and your daughter."

Wads rattled in with a Partridge Family tray on which rode Melmac cups, spoons, and the pan of water. He set it all on his coffee table—a cabinet door that straddled two plastic milk crates—and splashed hot water into the cups. A tea bag bobbed to the top of each.

Wads settled on a plastic chair shaped like hand. "So why come to me?"

Naseri stared at Larson.

"Shatha, Barb's a friend of the best kind. She can keep secrets."

"And you know this how?"

"She's a bartender." He passed a cup and spoon to Naseri seated kitty-corner from him on his couch. "Why me?"

"Raheem, he said if he should die, you would find the person who took his life." She brought a thumb drive from her pocket and held the drive out.

Wads raised an eyebrow. "What's this?"

"Raheem said you would know."

Larson took the thumb drive from Naseri and passed it to Wads. "The only way you're gonna find out what's on this is to plug it into your computer."

He shook the drive in his hand, like dice, as he got up and went to his laptop on a milk-crate table next to the window. Wads snatched a look outside—a peaceful night, as it should be at two in the morning, except for the little yapper in the yard across the street. A cat must have set him off.

Wads booted up the machine. When he had a screen, he plugged the drive in. "What am I going to see here?"

Naseri set her tea aside. "I do not know. Raheem only said it is important."

He leaned forward. Wads maneuvered the cursor around, clicking on one item, then the next. "Seems to be some kind of spreadsheet, and there are other files here. Hmm, bank stuff. And I'm supposed to see something in these figures? We've got derivatives here. I never did understand those things."

Larson came over. She hunched down, her breath warm on Wads's ear as she read over his shoulder. She tapped a jewel-studded fingernail on the screen. "That's yield, isn't it?"

"Appears so."

"I've got to buy some of that. Hold that for a while, I'd never have to work again."

"With the economy in the toilet, Barb, ehh." He wobbled his hand.

She riffled his hair. "Sweetie, you lost your farm. I didn't."

"Uh-huh. I think I've got to get my old accountant out at the Farm Credit to go over this. Shatha?"

"Yes?" She rose and came across the room as Wads turned to her. Glass shattered and she fell.

Wads bolted from his chair. He came down on his knees next to Naseri, sucked in wind when he saw blood escaping from a wound in her temple. He glanced up to Larson, croaked out, "Nine-One-One, now."

Wads up, hunched low. He skittered to the couch, pitched a cushion aside, recovered his nine mil, and raced out the apartment door. He galloped down the stairs three steps at a time, his bunny slippers slapping his heels. At the door, a bullet chipped a hole in the side glass.

Wads whipped the door open. He dropped to his belly, his gun aimed out.

A muzzle flash sparked in the window of a car across the street.

Wads answered the flash with a volley as the car screeched away—what kind of car? Dark? A foreign job? Wads ran into the street, craning for a better look as blue lights and a siren came around the corner behind him. And a second siren.

He raised his hands. Wads let his pistol dangle for all to see, one finger hooked through the trigger guard.

CHAPTER 7

WADS SAT ON THE HOOD of an unmarked cruiser while sheriff's Detective Howard Zigman stood with a cluster of city police on the front lawn, comparing notes. He came away.

"Wads, I don't know how you do it, but everywhere you've gone today, a dead body."

"Not at the Owls' Club."

"Karns is going to sue you, you know that?"

"For what?"

"Running over his motorcycle."

"Did you see any damage to my truck to support a wild claim like that?"

"The bashed-in door."

"You know where that's from."

"All right, enough. Look, I'm here as your friend, and I've got to tell you the city police want to arrest you."

"On what charge?"

"Discharging a firearm inside the city limits."

"Would they rather I be dead?"

"No. By the way, I like your bunny slippers."

Wads peered off to the side. "When am I gonna get my gun back?"

"You know the drill. Ballistics takes a couple days, even though they know you didn't shoot the woman in your apartment. Missus Naseri, what was she doing here?"

"Said she thought I could find the man who killed her husband."

"That's my job. You're not a sworn peace officer."

"I would be if you'd get me on with the sheriff's department."

"She have anything for you?"

"Not even a guess."

"Is that what Barb Larson's going to say? City detective says she's upstairs."

"You'll have to ask her."

"What's she doing here, anyway?"

"She knew I had a bad day, so she came over to hold my hand."

"Don't smart mouth me."

"Look, we were in the shower together, all right?"

"That I didn't need to know."

"Howard, you are such a prude."

"And my wife likes it that I am. So go over it for me."

Wads stared at Zigman. "All right, some assailant shoots Shatha through the window of my apartment. I run out with my gun. He shoots at me and I shoot at him."

"Six times. Yes, they counted your shell casings. You hit him?"

"I hit a window. I know because there's glass in the street. Maybe a door or the rear fender as he careened the hell out of here, but not him."

"Are you sure? The lighting out here's pretty bad."

"Howard, if I hit him, he'd be in a hospital with a hole in him or he'd be dead."

CHAPTER 8

A TANKER TRUCK, at the side of the Kwik Trip, dumped gasoline in the convenience store's underground tanks while Wads, his fists parked on his hips, stared at a waste barrel by the pumps. He called to his tall cashier, Cindy, squeegeeing the glass of the store's front door, "I thought the day shift was supposed to empty these things before they went off."

"Maybe they got busy."

"Aw cripes." He punched the overflow down and tied off the top of the trash bag before he hauled it out of the barrel. A Lexus LS 600 rolled up to the closest pump as Wads grubbed around the barrel's bottom for a new bag.

The driver stepped out. He swiped his card. "Looking for money down there?"

"Wouldn't complain if I found a fifty." Wads shook out the new bag. He tucked the excess around the outside edge of the barrel. "See you've got a new ride there, Mister Barnard."

"How many years have we known each other? Call me Ralph."

"All right, Ralph."

Barnard, in a suit and overcoat that matched the quality of his car, and a Tom Selleck mustache, triggered gas into the Lexus's filler pipe. "Had this sweet thing for three weeks. Figured it's time to fill up."

"Oh, one of those gas electrics."

"I've gone green. I heard you had a bit of excitement last night."

"More than a bit." Wads slung the trash bag over his shoulder.

"Do you think the man who killed that Naseri woman and shot at you also killed the woman's husband yesterday? He was one of my accountants, you know."

"You'll have to ask the police on that. Raheem working on anything special for you?"

"Routine stuff. I hired him because you said I should. An awful good man. I liked him and his wife and their little girl. Real sweet people. Friends are looking after the girl, right?"

"That's what I understand."

"Well, I set up a trust for her."

"Ralph, that's generous."

"It's the least I could do." Barnard put the nozzle back in the pump. "Are you arranging the funerals?"

"Digger will get the bodies after the autopsies. He and I'll work with the As-Sunnah imam to make sure we do everything right."

"I want you to give me the bills. Wads, I'm sure the Naseris didn't have any insurance."

"Again, that's generous."

"Well, I owe these people. We all do. If you'll excuse me, I've got to be on my way—community concert board tonight." He slid onto the leather driver's seat and whisked away, the car silent as an owl on the wing.

Wads headed for the dumpster near the tanker. The tankwagon driver clicked off the filler hose and pulled it up as Wads came by, splashing a slug of gasoline on him, startling Wads who dropped his trash bag. It burst, spilling the mess out everywhere.

The driver gaped. "I'm sorry."

"Arnie, just don't light a cigarette."

CHAPTER 9

WADS GLANCED at the antique Miller's beer clock over the bar as he sauntered into The Library, the lady gliding on a floral swing beneath the clock.

Twelve-ten.

He dropped his parka and cap in a leather chair and flopped in another, waggled two fingers to Barb, his signal for the usual.

She, in a red velvet top and black shorts, came over with a bottle of Muscle Milk–strawberry flavor. Her nose wrinkled as she came near.

Wads stared at her. "What?"

"You stink."

"Of gasoline, I know. Do you welcome all your customers this way?"

"Only the ones that stink."

"Hey, the tankwagon driver splashed me."

"So you stank up the store all night?"

"I guess."

She set the bottle on Wads's table. He twisted the top off the Muscle Milk and tossed back a slug.

"I'll tell you this, big boy, if this bar weren't smoke-free, you'd go up with a spark from someone's Bic."

"You make me feel so good."

"You ought to go home and take a bath."

"Can't. The water's off in my building."

She reached inside her bra and produced a key. She pressed it into his hand. "My place. Use my tub."

WADS TRUDGED up the final flight of stairs. He liked old Victorian houses, but a third-floor apartment—anyway, the key worked.

He felt for a light switch, unsurprised when he found it was the push kind. Wads pressed it and a chandelier came on, a soft light made softer by the ruby crystals dangling from the fixture. A walk around his apartment in a plain-Jane building a couple blocks away told company the furnishings were a mixture of old college dorm and Ikea while this was Bed, Bath & Beyond.

He found his way to the bathroom and turned on a spigot on a claw-foot tub, the tub a neat old thing. His grandparents had had one in their house.

Wads shucked himself out of his boots and clothes.

Ooo, stinky, stinky, stinky. There's gotta be a washer around somewhere.

He padded out into the hallway and opened doors until he found a laundry room. Wads pitched his clothes in the washing machine, poured in a shot of liquid Tide, and hit the start button.

That done, he padded back to the bathroom and eased himself down into the tub. Ahh, comfort, but where's the soap? A couple plastic bottles rested on a tray at the side of the tub. Wads helped himself to one—okay, liquid soap. He squeezed out a handful and lathered up. His nose vibrated. Wads turned the label and read it. Ohmigod, bubble bath—Midnight Pomegranate. And the other bottle? Shampoo—Lord, avocado and kumquat.

WADS STOOD at the pedestal basin, a plum-colored towel wrapped around his waist. He studied the face that looked back from the mirror, rubbed at the sandpaperish beard, more an eleven o'clock shadow than a five o'clock. He couldn't go to work like that, and no water at home—hmm.

Wads opened the medicine cabinet, and there on the bottom shelf laid a razor. He picked it up—gad, a Lady Schick—and a can of shaving foam. Lady Schick, just had to be.

If old Sergeant Baker saw me now, the ragging I'd get. Well, he's not here.

So Wads turned the hot water on in the basin. While the sink filled, he gazed around. Liquid soap. Yup, this time it really was. The label, Vanilla Brown Sugar. Oh jeez.

Small pictures on the wall, in a grouping to the side—two little kids, one in cowboy garb, the other dressed as a pirate with a scar and beard painted on with makeup. Who could they be? Barb had never mentioned children, and there sure weren't any signs of kids in the apartment—no toys or rubber duckies or Spiderman toothpaste.

Well, a mystery for another time.

He turned the water off and set to lathering up. The first stroke with the razor snagged skin. Wads grimaced. He tore off a piece of toilet paper and patted it over the wound, to stop the blood leak. Another nick on the next stroke and another dab of TP.

Wads threw out the blade. He replaced it with a new one from the cabinet.

And smooth shaving.

Done, he washed off the excess foam and wiped his face dry as a key scratched in the apartment door's lock.

A female voice called out, "It's only me. You decent?"

"In here."

The bathroom door opened. Larson shelled herself out of her coat as she came in. She looked at Wads's reflection in the mirror and laughed.

"What's so funny?"

"The toilet paper. My dad used to do that when he'd cut himself. He'd come out of the bathroom many a morning with four or five of those battle patches as he called them. He was always trying to get one more shave out of a blade that didn't have one more shave in it."

Wads held up the razor. "This worn-out blade was yours."

"Sorry. My, such interesting scars." Larson played her fingers along white welts under Wads's arm, the scars going down toward his waist.

"Souvenirs from Iraq," he said. "I've got some you can't see."

"Where?" She took hold of the towel.
"Hey now–"
Larson whipped it away.

CHAPTER 10

WADS STROLLED into the Farm Credit Agency where he rapped on the door frame of Ed Velstrum's office.

Velstrum, a decade older than Wads but with gray hair and worry lines that made him look two decades older, glanced up from a stack of spreadsheets.

"Eddie, I need your help."

"From what I hear, Wads old buddy, you don't need me. You need a bodyguard. You've got a killer and Barb Larson after you, and I don't know which is worse."

"Barb's not so bad."

"Aggressive as all hell when she's got a guy in her sights, and, you, my friend, you're it."

Wads waved a thumb drive.

Velstrum peered at it. "So what help do you expect from me? I couldn't save you from financial ruin."

"You understand numbers far better than I do."

"Daffy Duck understands numbers better than you do."

"Just can't pass the chance to gig me, can you? Look, there's stuff on here that I don't know what it is."

Velstrum waggled his fingers, and Wads came in. He passed the drive to the accountant.

Velstrum plugged the drive into his computer. "This better be good. I've got a headache."

"You've had a headache since Two thousand Three."

"The Iraq war. Hell of it is I didn't even get there. A damn concussion grenade blew out one of my eardrums in training." He squinted at the screen. "Bunch of files here. Which one do you want me to look at first?"

Wads leaned over Velstrum's shoulder. He tapped an icon.

Velstrum sniffed at the air. "You smell kind of fruity, my friend. What you been into?"

"I'm going to pass on that one."

The accountant hunched forward. He studied the page of data that flicked up on his screen. Velstrum scrolled down every few moments, humming to himself. He raised an eyebrow. "The code for this company, I recognize it. It's called America Invests. Buddy boy, what you've got here is a spreadsheet, shows the return over time on some pretty sophisticated instruments."

"How sophisticated?"

"You a physics PhD?"

"No."

"Neither am I. But as you say, I know numbers. See this, here, here, and here? A.I. has been giving its investors ten percent a year for a decade. Market doesn't work that way."

Wads stared at Velstrum. "A scam?"

"Who's behind A.I.?"

"How would I know?"

"So where did you get the thumb drive?"

"From the widow of an accountant who worked for Ralph Barnard's bank."

"Ah, yes, I always thought old Ralphie was a little too slick. Wads, you gotta take this to somebody who goes elephant hunting with a cannon."

CHAPTER 11

WADS SAT AT HIS DESK in the Kwik Trip's office, poring over the next week's work schedule with Cindy, his night clerk. He plugged an ear as he hollered at the hefty man standing on a chair in the corner, "Twigs, you have to make so much racket?"

"Do you want your closed-circuit TV repaired or not?"

"Repaired."

"Then don't bitch."

"But do you have to use a ballpeen hammer?"

"Sometimes these covers need a little persuading before they'll jump back in place."

Twigs Kushmerick whanged the cabinet again. "There, done."

He got down and, as he did, he hitched up his pants threatening to fall to his ankles. "Wanna see if we got a picture?"

"That's why Kwik Trip's paying you the big bucks."

"Damn right it is. Double time plus travel." Kushmerick punched a button on the panel of monitors. A flickering travelled across the series of screens followed by pictures—the pumps, the front door, the area in front of the cash register. A hairy form came ambling through the front door.

Wads rocked back in his chair, his hands cupped behind his head. "Is that what I think it is?"

The screen from the camera behind the cash register showed a gorilla moving around the store, examining the Ding Dongs and Ho Hos.

Cindy stifled a giggle. "I could believe this if it was Halloween."

The gorilla turned to the banana display. He glanced over his shoulder, then grabbed the giant Kwik Trip banana that advertised bananas thirty-nine cents a pound and ran out.

Wads hooted.

Twigs gathered up his tools. "You don't know who that is, do ya?"

"Probably some kid from the college stealing advertising stuff for his dorm room."

"Didn't you see the story on the TV news last night?"

"We were working, Twigs."

"That's the by-damn Banana Bandit. He hit four stores in Madison last week and now yours. You gotta call Nine-One-One."

"You think the cops are gonna believe this? I'm not sure I do."

"Hey, thank you to my hard work, Wads, you got it on tape."

Cindy chortled some more. "I think we should put this up on YouTube."

A black car drove into the picture coming from a camera focused on pumps Three and Four. The driver stepped out. He ratcheted his ball cap down and strode toward the front door. The next screen picked up a hand movement, the man pulling a pistol from beneath his jacket.

Wads reached for a button under his desk. He mashed it, setting off a wailing siren, like a police car's.

CHAPTER 12

WADS, HIS SHOULDERS SAGGING beneath his mackinaw, shambled into The Library, his shift at the convenience store over.

"How you doing, big guy?" Larson called to him from behind the bar. She dipped a shot glass in sudsy water as she gave him a smile that said I've got something special for you. "Want to use my tub again?"

Wads came up to the bar. He leaned on it and beckoned Larson in close. "Your tub? Hell, no. One night of sex on the bathroom floor is all I can take."

"We can move to my bedroom."

He threw up his hands.

She pointed to a man in a corner booth, his back to them. "You've got company."

"What's he drinking?"

"He says Baptist gin."

"Damn, it's Zigman. Gimme a Coke—"

"And your usual, I know." Barb brought a can of Coca Cola and a bottle of Muscle Milk up from the under-bar fridge. She handed them to Wads.

He took them and went over to the far booth where he slid onto a vacant bench seat. Wads shoved the Coke across the table. "Thought you might need a new one."

Zigman, as cadaverously thin as ever, grinned. "Ahh, you warm my heart."

"You do know what that stuff's doing to your plumbing, don't you? I use Coke to eat the corrosion off battery terminals." Wads made a fizzing sound, his fingers dancing up in an imitation of a cloud of smoke rising.

The sheriff's detective sipped from the can, then smacked his lips as he resumed his grin. "Like it anyway. Understand a man with a gun came into your store tonight, my friend, after the gorilla stole your big banana. Saw that last one on YouTube."

"You?"

"My kid told me about it. So the gunner, you've got something he wants, don't you?"

"What makes you think that?"

"City cops told me what they saw on your videotape—black Mercury, no license plates, man with a cap pulled down. This is a pro. He knew he was going to be on camera."

Wads chewed on the inside of his lip.

"So what is it? Evidence of some kind, have I got that right?"

"I can't tell you."

"Thumb drive? Don't look so surprised. Barb let it slip."

"Zig, if I were to give the drive to you or the city cops, you'd screw it up. I've got to take this to the state attorney general. We dated once. I've already called her."

"I could get a search warrant."

"Do you think I've stashed it anywhere where you could find it?"

Zigman worked his fingers over his chin as he studied Wads. "So when and where do you meet with the A.G.?"

"And have you there?"

"I could tail you."

Wads laughed. "After a hard night at the store, buddy, I needed a little humor."

CHAPTER 13

WADS CHECKED HIS CELL for the time as he came out of his apartment building—four o'clock. Overcast, the feel of snow imminent. He pulled the collar of his mack up around his ears, protection from the norther whistling down the street.

He unlocked his truck, and, just before he got in, gave a wave to a rusty brown Chevrolet a half-block down the street.

Wads luxuriated in the warmth of the cab after he settled in. He gave a silent thank you to the dealer who had insisted he get a remote starter on his then new truck. Fire up the engine while you're still finishing your grapefruit, he had said.

Wads drove off, adjusting his mirror as he did. The brown Chev—the sheriff department's stakeout car, he'd seen it before—was there, following. He knew who had to be at the wheel—Zigman.

Wads waited until he passed the city limits sign on the road to Lake Kandiyah before he stepped the gas pedal to the floor. The driver of the brown car had to have done the same. Wads chuckled as he watched the image in his mirror. And there was a second image further back, no more than the size of the tip of his little finger—a second car, black.

For Wads, it was all in the timing. Ahead, the lights on a railroad crossing gate began to flash. He held his speed. Wads shot across the tracks as the arms came down and watched Zigman slow and swerve between the crossing arms, falling behind in the chase.

Wads tapped his brakes. He let his speed play off as he came up on a curve, then powered through, through that one and the next. Wads hit the brakes, this time hard. He skidded his truck off onto an unplowed township road that led into a thick stand of burr oaks.

A drift. He slammed into it, and the air bags burst out of their restraints. They pinned him as the truck rocked to a stop. The moment the bags deflated, Wads threw open the door. He grabbed a coil of rope from the floor on the passenger side, slung it over his shoulder, and plunged off into the deep interior of the woods. There he found it, the Arctic Cat snowmobile. He'd driven it in a dozen hours before. A twist of the ignition key and the engine came alive. Wads mounted up. He rode the Cat out of the woods at an easy speed, took his leisure as he drove toward the shore of Kandiyah Lake. Zigman would find his truck, Wads knew it. He would hear the snowmobile and back out to the county road and come after him. Part two of the plan.

As Wads rolled out onto the snow-covered ice, he glanced to the side, at the brown Chev barrelling down toward the lake at a helluva speed. Wads twisted the throttle full wide, and the Cat responded. It threw up a rooster tail of white as it tore away into the gloom, out onto ice blown free of snow.

He hazarded a look back and the lost his pea cap to the wind for his effort. The Chev was there, closing the gap.

Wads hunkered low. He fought the blast ripping at his face and hair, zeroed his focus on a dark band ahead—open water he'd seen the previous day. The band veered to either side of his course. He'd never done it before, but Crazy Bill had—told him about it over a root beer at the Kwik Trip. At the last moment, Wads stood up. He hauled up on the handlebars, believing maybe it would help, and he and the Cat found themselves over the water, the Cat's engine howling, the snowmobile's track spinning free of any hard contact with a solid world.

The Cat hit the water like a skipping stone, skipped three more times and out onto the ice on the far side.

Wads braked. He threw his snowmobile into a sideward slide and watched the brown Chev go into a slide of its own on the Jimmytown side of the open water, watched the car laze into a three-sixty and swoosh in.

The driver burst from the door.

Wads grabbed his rope. He ran to the edge of the ice, planted himself, and spun the loop end of the rope out like a lariat. He let the loop float out and down around the sheriff's detective flailing in the black water. Wads gave a jerk that tightened the loop, then, pulling hand over hand, hauled Zigman to solid ice and out.

Zigman spat water. "What the hell are you doing?"

"Saving your life. You can't swim any better than a rock. Jeezus, man, I figured you knew about the water and go around. And I'd lose you good."

Zigman, shivering, shucked himself out of the rope. He threw it aside and twisted back to the water, its surface roiling with great bubbles of air escaping from the sinking car. "How'm I gonna explain this to the sheriff?"

"I'll help you, but not today." Wads aimed a gloved hand at the shore they'd left behind, at a black car parked there, its running lights on. "Bad company. Let's get out of here before he figures out what to do next."

He hurried Zigman to the snowmobile. After he helped the soggy, chilled detective onto the rear of the seat, they roared off for the far shore, the Cat's engine screaming.

The first flakes of a new snow—the flakes small and buckshot hard—came out of the clouds. The norther drove the pellets at a slant, and they stung the side of Wads's face. He squinted his windward eye tight shut and held course until the snowmobile shot up on the far shore, into an open area near a lake cabin. Wads stopped the machine by the door and helped Zigman off, Zigman moving with the stiffness of an old man.

"End of the line for you, buddy." Wads reached above the door ledge. The reach produced a key, and he unlocked the door, horsed Zigman inside. The place smelled of must and rancid bacon fat. "Netty Testaman's shack. Not exactly a neat housekeeper she. You get yourself a fire going and call someone to come for you."

Wads laid his cell on a table as shabby as the cabin, but before he could turn, Zigman's quaking hand clamped onto his arm. "Where you going?"

"Zig, you know I can't tell you that." He pried Zigman's hand away. Wads ran for the door. He slammed it behind him and jumped aboard the Cat.

Wads sped off, back out onto the ice. He paralleled the shore for a quarter of a mile before he turned off a second time. Wads plowed the Cat up onto the shore, toward a structure that was little more than a shanty with a lean-to attached. He drove the Cat under the covering, cut the engine, and slogged away through snow up to his knees.

After some minutes, he came out on a county road. A Suzuki X-90, older than he, sat idling on the shoulder. The window rolled down, and Barb Larson leaned out.

"Going my way, big boy?"

Wads shoe-horned himself into the passenger seat. A spring prodded his butt, and he rounced around until he got comfortable. "Some car you got here. My granddad's city brother had a Nash Metropolitan. I ever tell you that? This car isn't any bigger than his was."

"On a bartender's salary it's all I can afford, so don't complain."

"I'm not."

"All right. Where to?"

"Madison."

Larson stepped down on the accelerator, and the engine coughed a couple times before it smoothed out. She twisted the wiper switch to ON. That set the wipers to thumping away at the snow pellets bouncing off the windshield.

Wads peered at his driver, her face illuminated by the glow from the instrument panel. "I gotta ask."

"The answer is yes," she said.

"You haven't heard the question."

"The answer's still yes." Larson grinned through her concentration on her driving. "So when do you want the wedding?"

"Barb!"

"That's not the question?"

"No. Those pictures of kids in your bathroom."

"Oooh. My boy and girl." She flicked on the clicker—the turn signal—slowed, and turned onto the Interstate entrance ramp. She again stepped down on the accelerator. "I lost them in the divorce. The judge didn't think much of me being a bartender."

"So you see them?"

"One weekend a month." She peered up into the mirror at headlights behind her. "Come on, fella, you can pass me."

Wads twisted around. He stared out the back window. "He is kinda close."

"Just came up on me when we got on the I-road."

"So pick up your speed."

"Huh-uh. I don't even like driving this fast when it's snowing."

"All right, slow down then. Force him to pass you."

Larson took her foot off the gas pedal. "He's slowing, too."

"Guess we'll have to live with him then."

She resumed her speed.

Wads, rather than settle back, continued to watch over his shoulder. Lights at a truck weigh station ahead radiated out through the snow. "Now we'll see who he is."

The Suzuki passed under the lights as did the car behind.

"Oh shit."

Larson, startled, glanced at Wads.

He drummed his fingertips on the dash. "Bad company."

"What bad company?"

"The guy who killed Shatha and shot at me. That's his car."

"You sure?"

"No license plate, at least not on the front."

"Well, my car's got all the oomph of a motorscooter, so we're sure not gonna out-run him."

Wads raked his fingers back through his hair. "You got your cellphone?"

"Sure, in my purse."

He hauled Larson's purse, the size of a valise, out of the gap between the seats. Wads mined for some moments, his desperation increasing as he sorted through makeup, spare clothing, and the booty from a quick stop at the video store. At last, he came up with the phone. Wads punched in Seven-Seven-Eight and waited through a couple buzzes before a gravelly voice said, "State Police."

Wads glanced over his shoulder as he jabbered at the phone. "The missus an' me, we're on the Interstate, a couple miles north of the Stoughton Fifty-One exit."

"Yeah?"

"My God, man, you're not going to believe us, but there's what looks like a black Mercury ahead of us, northbound. And he's weaving. That's darn dangerous in this snow, you know. We're thinking maybe he's drunk."

"I've got a car near there. I'll dispatch him. Who is this?"

"A couple concerned citizens." He clicked off and put the phone back in the purse.

Larson kept her focus on the patch of road showing in her headlights. "Wads, you lie."

"Hey, it's the best I can do on short notice."

Blue lights ahead lit up the southbound lanes. A state trooper car shot by, tore through the median, and come roaring northward through the driving snow.

Wads laughed as he rubbed his hands. "I do love it when the cavalry arrives before the settlers get scalped."

The trooper car and the Mercury fell back, their headlights sliding off onto the shoulder.

Larson relaxed her grip on the steering wheel. "What if it isn't him?"

"Then it isn't. We'll never know. When we get on the Beltline, mind cutting off at South Towne?"

"You need something?"

"A new cell."

"What happened to yours?"

"Oh, I gave it to Zigman. His kinda got drowned."

"Do I want to know why?"

"Some night he'll tell you over a Baptist gin."

WADS TROTTED OUT of the Walmart, a Trak phone in hand. The wind hit him and he kicked up his pace, hurrying on to Larson's Suzuki idling in a handicapped spot. Something stopped him when he came around the rear of the car, to get to the passenger's door, something silver dangling from beneath the rear bumper.

Wads hunched down. He grabbed hold of an errant strip of duct tape and ripped it away. A small black object with a short antenna attached came with it. He opened the door and held the thing out to Larson.

She stared at it. "And I'm supposed to know what that is?"

"A transmitter. That's how the bastard tracked us to the Interstate. Bet there was one on my truck, too." Wads threw the miniature down. He crushed it hard under his boot heel before he got in the car.

"Well, we're rid of that," he said and gestured for Larson to take off.

She let out the clutch and zipped away, nodding to the side. "Black car there."

Wads turned. He gazed out the back window. "Mercury, all right, but a Romney/Ryan bumper sticker? I don't think it's our villain." He settled back with his new cell, and, as he did, someone rose up in the driver's seat of the Mercury.

Wads tapped away on his cell's keypad. "I'm gonna program your number into my phone and mine into yours. If we get separated, we can still be in contact."

Larson slowed for traffic, then slid onto the entrance to the Beltline. "You think that's gonna happen?"

"Boy Scout motto, be prepared." He keyed his number into Larson's cell. When he finished, he dropped it in her purse and pulled his military nine-mil out of his shoulder holster.

Larson stared at the gun, but only for a moment. A semi passed her, its wind blast buffeting her car, she wrestling with the steering wheel for control. Only when the driving smoothed out did Larson ask, "What's that for?"

"This?" Wads held up the pistol. "This is for growed-up Boy Scouts." He jacked a round into the firing chamber, clicked the safety on, and chucked the gun back in his holster.

Larson guided her car onto John Noland Drive. "I'm not going to get shot at, am I?"

"No."

"Can I hold you to that?"

Wads checked the time on his cell—five forty-five. "Nice thing about going to the Capitol at this time of day, not much traffic."

"I usually go the long way around, to East Washington and up."

"Today, how about you save a couple minutes? Cut off on Broom. A block to Wilson, a block to Hamilton, then shoot to the Square."

Larson nodded. She wheeled the Suzuki through the turns and up to the Capitol Square where she eased into the thin traffic rounding the Square. She slipped across to the inside lane. "Where do you want out?"

"Other side."

As Larson concentrated on making the first turn, Wads glanced to his right and sucked wind. A black car was there, the barrel of a gun thrust out the driver's window.

Wads whipped his foot across to the brake pedal of Larson's Suzuki. He stomped hard.

Larson, thrown forward, clung to the steering wheel. "You crazy?"

The black Mercury whistled past and spun around.

Wads shot a hand at the Capitol building. "Buck over the curb! Get me to a door."

Larson cranked the wheel. She banged the car up onto the sidewalk and the snow-covered lawn beyond, the Suzuki's wheels spinning, throwing up a mini-blizzard as the car hurtled toward the near corner of the Capitol. She glanced at her mirror.

Wads saw her look. "He's not after you. He's after me."

"What's that mean?"

"It means get outta here after I bail out."

He shoved the door open as Larson racked the Suzuki's speed down. Wads flung himself out. He rolled, scrambled to his feet, and hop-ran for the massive oak doors. Wads plunged inside and down a nearly dark hallway.

His cell went off.

Wads slid into a side hallway as he dug out his phone. He hit the incoming number.

Larson's voice came through, chocked with panic. "He's in the building."

"Call the police." Wads pocketed his phone. He drew his pistol and leaned around the corner.

A dark figure came charging his way.

Wads banged off a shot, and the figure spun into a doorway.

"Who are you?" Wads called out.

"Why should I tell you?"

"I'd like to know who's trying to kill me."

"That's fair."

"So?"

"They call me the vacuum cleaner."

"That's a helluva name."

"People hire me to suck up their messes. Think about it."

"So I'm somebody's mess?"

"Quite right."

Who says quite right? Wads desperately wanted to grab a look around the corner—to see who the man was—but he also wanted to keep his head. "Whose mess am I?" he asked.

"Sorry. Professional ethics."

Wads glanced down at his knee. For the first time he saw the rip in his pant leg and the red stain. "Let me guess. Ralph Barnard."

Something that sounded like plastic hit the marble floor. It made a rolling sound. Wads ventured a peek. He swore and ran for a near staircase up. Gotta get the high ground.

Behind him the something popped, and the hallway filled with gas.

CHAPTER 14

HIGH GROUND, gotta get the high ground.

The thought hammered at Wads as he pounded past the second-floor landing for the third floor, and only at the top did he realize that the sound of his boots on the hard marble had given him away. He ripped his boots off and threw them aside.

"Hey, don't mess up my hallway."

Wads swivelled around, his pistol out, to face a janitor. She dropped her mop.

"Look, lady, I'm not gonna hurt you. Just get outta here, someplace where you can lock yourself in and call the police."

"What's going on?"

"Lady, someone's trying to kill me, and I don't need you in the way. Now go." He waved his pistol toward a far hallway, and the janitor, her hair pulled back under a Brewers ball cap, sprinted off.

Wads grabbed the woman's cart. He pulled the two trash barrels from it, flopped them in front of the staircase a half step in. He latched onto the mop and swung it at an overhead light, smashing it. Wads then scattered the janitor's squeegees and dusters and spilled her bucket of soapy wash water over the floor. He pitched the bucket down the stairs and ran for the rotunda balcony.

Behind him someone fell across the barrels and swore, slipped in the wash water and fell a second time.

Wads raced on in a limp-run around the balcony to the far side. Just as he plunged into a new hallway, he heard a sound—like a cheap firecracker—and felt a bee sting in his side. He whipped around.

On the side of the balcony from which Wads had come, a man in a black ball cap laid across the broad banister, sighting along the barrel of his weapon.

Wads dropped. The firecracker again, and a bullet gouged a chunk out of a bronze bust of 'Fighting' Bob La Follette, to Wads's side and three feet up.

A voice that had the sound of the Grim Reaper came across the way. "Gotcha with the first shot, didn't I?"

Wads fingered his side, and his hand showed blood. He gazed around the rotunda balcony, studying the walls. "Vacuum Cleaner, you any good at billiards?"

"Why the question?"

"Humor me. You any good at billiards?"

"Chess. Chess is my game."

Wads turned. He aimed forty-five degrees at the circular wall. "Three bank shot, eight ball in the side pocket." He squeezed the trigger, heard the ricochets and an "uhnn."

"Even-up now?" Wads asked.

"I'm dying."

"I'm good at a blind shot, but not that good." He crawled away, to another staircase.

Gotta get myself to the high ground.

WADS PULLED HIMSELF onto a fourth-floor landing. He worked his way back into the rotunda. There he peered through the banister, down to the balcony below, and jerked back as three shots chipped away at the marble supports.

"The shooting's up there!"

"Yeah, I see' im. Police! Put down your weapon."

Voices from below.

Then a shot and a volley of gunfire.

When it ceased, Wads again peered between the spindles. He aimed his pistol at the spot where the shooter should be.

Jeez, where'd he go?

Something pressed on Wads's back, and a husky voice said, "Put yer gun on the floor. Push it away from you."

"Uncle Harley?"

"Wads?"

Wads turned his head as best he could. From the corner of his eye, he saw standing over him a man with a face chiselled from granite and a bush of white hair, blue shirt, sleeves pushed above the elbows, necktie pulled loose. The man held a shotgun, its single barrel jammed against Wads's spine.

Wads gave a jerk of his jaw. "What the hell are you doing?"

"What the hell are you doing?"

"Trying to keep myself alive. There's a guy out to kill me before I can get to the A.G.'s office. What're you doing here, anyway?"

Harley Wadkowski took a step back. He swung his twelve-gauge to the side. "My office's just down the hall. Workin' late for my Sauk County constituents when I hear all this blastin' goin' on."

Wads pressed a hand against his side as he got to his knees. With his free hand he recovered his pistol.

"You hurt, son?" Wadkowski asked.

"Just a nick. Thank God the cavalry's come."

"City police, yeah, I called 'em. And the state police, too."

"Unc, standing up like that, you could get your head blown off."

"Oh for cripes sake." The legislator hunkered down next to Wads. "What do we do now?"

"Either wait for the cops to catch him or go hunting."

"Personally, I'm for huntin'. I'm a damn good bird man."

"Any chance he could take an elevator to the basement and get out of here?"

"We lock the elevators at six."

A door across the way inched open. The shooter crouched in the doorway.

Like duck hunters from a blind, both Wadkowskis popped up. They let loose with a hail of bullets and buckshot.

The shooter fell.

Wads and his uncle raced around the balcony. As they did, the man crawled to a side door. He pushed it open, hauled himself over the sill, and kicked the door shut.

The Wadkowskis slid on blood on the marble floor, the senior Wadkowski slamming down hard. But he held onto his shotgun.

"You all right?" Wads asked.

"Gonna have to see my chiropractor. Waddy, we got him if he's leakin' like this."

"Gimme your shotgun."

"Why?"

"My gun's empty."

Wads pulled his uncle up and relieved him of his twelve gauge. He pumped a new shell into the firing chamber.

"I'm coming with you, boy."

"Hell you are. Where's this door go?"

"Up to the inside observation decks. He's not gonna trap himself. My bet is he'll go up to one of the three doors that go outside."

Wads eased the door open. He leaned through, saw a blood trail in the dim light from a wall sconce, the trail going toward the stairs. Wads glanced up.

Nothing.

Only silence.

He limped up the first set of steps—marble—to the fifth-floor landing. The blood trail did not go toward the exterior door, but toward the next staircase. The up arrow said Museum and Trumpeter's Ring.

Fourteen steps and the sixth-floor landing. A circular staircase ahead. To the side, an exterior door and blood droplets going that way.

Wads opened the door. He stepped out into the snow and pressed his back against the wall. "Cleaner man," he called out.

"Come after me and you die."

The voice had a distant sound and seemed to come from above.

Wads peered up. "I could leave you out here, bolt the door. You'll freeze by morning if you don't bleed out before that."

"I know you, John Wads. You can't wait that long."

"You got that right."

Wads inched to the side, to a ladder, his foot brushing against a container. He picked it up. A milk chug. Only no milk, just a splash of something red.

He pitched the chug over the side and snaked his way up the rungs of the ladder. At the top, Wads poked his head up just enough that he could see statuary high and to his right, and the columned walkway around the Trumpeter's Ring—the columns supporting the Capitol's exterior dome—the walkway where someone could make his way to the far side, but why?

"Fake blood," Wads called out.

"You found my bottle." The voice, though faint, sliced through the wind.

"Body armor?" Wads asked.

"Where it counts. Gives me the edge, don't you think?"

Wads clung to the ladder. The rungs cut into the soles of his stockinged feet as he peered in the direction from which he'd heard the shooter.

"Coming after you?" Wads called out. "I'm reconsidering."

"Reconsider too long and I'm gone."

Shoot. The observation deck on the roof of the north wing. A two-story drop, but a man could make it, even wounded.

Wads hauled himself up onto the Trumpeter's Ring.

Go left?

Would he be there, waiting to kill me?

Wads glanced that way, then set out in the other direction, the wind whipping his hair as he shuffled along, shotgun at the ready. His socks, wet from the snow, so frozen that Wads could no longer feel his feet.

Yet he went on, a cluster of statues ahead.

The high ground.

Yes, that was the high ground.

Wads pulled himself up and in among the statues, short of the north wing. The edge of the blast of light from the observation deck's floods illuminated his position, the blast that bathed the dome and Lady Wisconsin—the Golden Lady—at the pinnacle of the structure that topped the dome. The light seared Wads's eyes, and he squinted, squinted through the dazzle of snow crystals driven sideways by the wind, squinted until he made out the shooter in half-silhouette, crouched on the banister below, the shooter peering down at the observation deck.

Wads leaned across the lap of a seated Greek scholar studying a scroll. He brought up his shotgun and sighted along the barrel. "You can't jump fast enough."

The shooter, his pistol out, twisted towards Wads.

Wads responded, squeezed the trigger.

The shotgun's firing pin hammered the center of the brass end of the shell in the chamber. The shell's powder exploded and rocketed out a tight fist of steel pellets.

CHAPTER 15

WADS, STRIPPED TO THE WAIST, sat amidst a litter of law journals on a coffee table in the state attorney general's office, a parka-clad EMT taping a patch over his wound.

The EMT smoothed the tape. "You're darn lucky. Tore through muscle, not the abdominal cavity."

The A.G., Constance Herr, as attractive as when she represented the state in the Miss Universe contest fifteen years earlier–attractive even in a blue business suit–glanced away from her computer screen. "So my old boyfriend's going to survive?"

"I don't see why not?"

"Don't make any record of this and don't tell anybody you've been here."

"But there's paperwork–"

"Paperwork, hell, young man. I've already issued an order holding the Nine-One-One call tapes for a grand jury. You do as I say or I'll have you jailed for interfering."

He shrugged and packed his kit and left.

Herr, who knew when to charm and when to be the tough law enforcer, turned to Wads. "You know I'm stepping in deep manure here."

"Why's that?"

"Ralph Barnard has raised a lot of money for my campaigns, and the governor's, too. We're going to get splashed. But by what I read here, Ralph is some bastard."

Wads reached for his shirt. "So what do you intend to do?"

"I've got a federal attorney who owes me a favor and a friend at the SEC I'll call."

"So you're going to arrest him?"

"Not until we get an indictment. The feds for fraud—guaranteed—and I'll go after him for murder for hire."

"How long'll this take?"

"A couple days."

"Connie, the TV people had to be listening to their police scanners. This is gonna get out, and Ralph's gonna get gone."

The A.G. shook her head. "No. The state police commandant'll put a lid on everything, and I've got a safe house where I can hide you."

Harley Wadkowski stepped away from a detail of troopers. "He's my nephew. How about I put him up?"

"Assemblyman, that's good with me. And, Harley—"

"Yes?"

"Take your shotgun home. If I ever hear it's in your office again, I'll confiscate it." She again turned to Wads. "I don't want you calling anybody, understand? You've disappeared."

Wads waggled a hand, as if to say ehh, then went back to buttoning his shirt.

"Tomorrow," Herr went on, "I'll have the state police put out a release stating you were killed in a shooting on the Capitol grounds. Let Mister Barnard think you're dead."

"But what about Barb Larson?"

"Who's that?"

"A friend. She drove me here."

"Let her think you're dead, too."

WADS AND HIS UNCLE left the attorney general's office, Wads padding along in blue footies. A trooper, coming their way, held up a pair of boots. "Found these down the hall. Figured you might want them."

Wads took the boots. He leaned against the wall and pulled them on, knelt and, glancing up at the trooper, laced them. "You look like you played football. College?"

"The U-dub."

"Tackle?"

"Guard." The trooper reached out his paw. He helped Wads up. "I'm Dan Blanowitz. I get to look after you for a while."

"The A.G.?"

"Yup."

A medical examiner's crew came off through the double doors from the observation deck. They pushed a gurney, a body in a black body bag strapped to it.

Wads stopped them. "Mind if I look?"

Blanowitz intervened before they could object. "We're attached to the A.G.'s office. It's okay."

One of the crew unzipped the bag, enough that Wads could see the face of the man who had intended to kill him. Wads leaned in, as did his uncle.

"Gawd, looks like hamburger," the senior Wadkowski said.

"I hit him with the full load. I intended to." Wads touched the arm of the nearest examiner. "Any identification?"

"Nothing in his pockets but a tin of Carmax. His face won't help us, but we did take his fingerprints and a DNA sample."

"Any wounds other than the face?"

"A couple pellets to the hands, and a lot of damage to his clothes. The guy was wearing Kevlar, the lightest I've ever seen. Front, but not the back."

Wads touched the body bag. "That would be important."

The examiner crewman's eyebrow rose, puzzlement apparent. "Do you know something?"

Wads shook his head.

"Well, when we rolled him, we found he'd been shot in the fanny. Odd, wouldn't you say?"

"Definitely." Wads winked at his uncle.

The crewman reached for the zipper pull. "You done?"

"Yeah. Thanks for letting me take a look."

He zipped up the bag, and he and his partners went on, pushing the gurney ahead of them.

The senior Wadkowski nudged his nephew. "The butt shot, that yours?"

"Uh-huh."

"You gonna tell 'em?"

"They wouldn't believe me, not how I did it. And I'm not sure I believe it either, except I was there. I heard the strike."

CHAPTER 16

WADS READJUSTED HIMSELF, uncomfortable in both the hard oak armchair and the suit he'd borrowed from his uncle, the suit one size too small. He faced a grand jury meeting in a plain-vanilla committee room.

Constance Herr, in dark slacks, cream-colored blouse, and a tailored red jacket, stood to Wads's side. She looked up from the notes on her legal pad. "Mister Wadkowski, would it surprise you that the bullet that killed Shatha Naseri—the wife of Raheem Naseri who was also murdered, the accountant who worked for Ralph Barnard—came from the same gun that an assailant used when he attempted to kill you?"

"No."

"Why is that?"

"I saw his car the night he killed Shatha, and I saw him with the car when he came to the Kwik Trip store I manage."

"And you were where at the time?"

"In the office. We were watching him on a video monitor. We'd just had it fixed."

"What happened?"

"He'd already shot at me once, so I triggered an alarm and he ran."

"Did you see his face?"

"Not clearly, no."

Herr went to the lectern. When she returned, she carried a photo which she handed to Wads. "Can you identify this person?"

"Ohmigod."

"So you know him. Fingerprints identify him as your assailant, as one Garth Kellogg."

Wads pulled at his earlobe. "No wonder he wouldn't give me his name."

"How do you know him?"

"He was in a Guard unit in Iraq. They loaned him to my military police company."

"And why would that be?"

"Kellogg had a special skill set that made him particularly valuable."

"He was an assassin, wouldn't it be right to say that?"

"Yes. When we'd identify an opposition commander we thought best be eliminated, we'd send him out. It was cheaper than a rocket and far less messy."

"Your Mister Kellogg, he did what you might call good work?"

"Until he began killing Iraqis who were important to us."

"So what happened?"

"The captain ordered my squad to hunt him down, kill him if necessary."

"And did you find him?"

"We thought so, dead in a house that had been booby-trapped. His body was badly torn up, but we found his wallet and dog tags. A DNA sample identified him. Had to have been tampered with now, I suppose."

"So he eluded you." Herr studied Wads. "Could his attempt at killing you be revenge?"

"I don't think so. He said I was a problem that he'd been hired to, in effect, clean up."

"Did he tell you who hired him?"

"No, so I asked if it was Ralph Barnard. He didn't deny it."

WADS AND HIS UNCLE stood at a window outside the committee room, gazing at the Capitol across the way, the late afternoon sun casting half the building in shadow.

Harley Wadkowski leaned against the frame. "So you knew this guy."

"A hundred years ago." Wads rubbed his side.

"And you never recognized him?"

"I suppose I should have known his voice, but I thought all this time he was dead. And I couldn't see his face well enough."

"Well, you don't have to beat yourself up."

Herr came out of the committee room, talking on her cell phone. She clicked off her call and conferred with Trooper Blanowitz, pointed him off toward the elevator and he left. Herr came over to Wads and his uncle.

She held up a folded paper. "We got it. Wads, your testimony was the clincher. The grand jury handed down a true bill."

"So now are you going to arrest Ralph?"

"Not just yet. The Milwaukee Symphony is playing a concert in the rotunda tonight, and I'm going. How would you like to be my guests?"

CHAPTER 17

THE TWO WADKOWSKIS, both in a tuxedos, stood next to the statue of one-time Wisconsin governor and senator, 'Fighting' Bob La Follette. They passed the time gassing about the weather until Trooper Blanowitz, in dress uniform, came up with Howard Zigman, the tall, lean detective from the Wappello County Sheriff's Department.

Zigman slapped Wads's shoulder. "My God, I didn't believe it when Blanny told me you were alive. Did you know Barb's planning your funeral?"

Wads tugged at his earlobe. "Guess she can call it off."

"She doesn't know?"

"They haven't let me near a phone."

"Ooo, she's gonna be upset, probably kill you so she can still have the funeral. She's got thirty-five bottles of Muscle Milk on the back bar—for your age—each with a crepe band."

"Oh Lordy. So what're you doing here?"

"Not sure. Blanny called me, told me to get my butt up here, lights and siren if I had to." Zigman gestured toward the orchestra tuning up at the north side of the rotunda. "Do you know if they'll be playing any Bach?"

Harley Wadkowski pulled down on his cummerbund. "I was hoping for some Willy Nelson."

Wads gave him a doleful look, then swivelled back to Zigman. "Howard, this is my Uncle Harley. Harley's a state assemblyman from Sauk County. Unc, Howard Zigman's a sheriff's detective and I guess maybe the best friend I've got."

"Assemblyman, I should arrest your nephew for dunking me in lake the other day."

Wads gave Zigman a one-armed hug. "Hey, buddy, I pulled you out."

"It was zero. I darn near froze."

"It was twenty-eight. I can't believe you were any more than just a tad chilly."

Blanowitz raised a hand. "Enough. Let's get seated." He guided Wads and his uncle into the third row. "The A.G.'s going to be behind, but don't turn around until she speaks to you. Understood?"

Wads waved his agreement.

Blanowitz and Zigman took seats in the fourth row, Blanowitz taking care to keep three seats open to the left of Zigman.

Moments later, Constance Herr, in a strapless maroon evening gown and a diamond necklace, entered the rotunda, Ralph Barnard at her side, he in a swallowtail tuxedo. She motioned him into the fourth row.

"It's a shame Elsa couldn't come," she said as she sat down. "Oh, there's someone here you should meet."

Herr tapped Wads's shoulder, and he twisted around.

Barnard gaped.

Wads winked at him. "Surprise. I haven't been buried just yet."

Herr picked it up. "Ralph, he testified before a grand jury today about your shooter, Garth Kellogg. The jury indicted you for conspiracy to commit murder and murder for hire."

"The hell you say."

"I do say." She motioned to Zigman. "Detective, do you have your handcuffs?"

Wads clapped Barnard on the shoulder. "Ralph, how are you at doing the perp walk?"

ABOUT THE AUTHOR

Jerry Peterson writes crime novels set in Kansas, Tennessee, and now with *Iced*, in Wisconsin.

Before becoming a writer, he taught speech, English, and theater in Wisconsin high schools, then worked in communications for farm organizations for a decade in Wisconsin, Michigan, Kansas and Colorado.

Peterson followed that with a decade as a reporter, photographer, and editor for newspapers in Colorado, West Virginia, Virginia, and Tennessee.

Today, he lives and writes in his home state of Wisconsin, the land of dairy cows, craft beer, and good books.

UPCOMING TITLES

Coming soon, *The Last Good Man*, the first book in my new series of Wings Over the Mountains novels. This is a mainstream novel. Pappy Brown, age 65, retires and goes to college.

That will be followed by *Capitol Crimes*, the second book in this series . . . a mystery.